# The Great Biscuit Bake-Off

Published by Disney Press, an imprint of Buena Vista Books, Inc. No part of
this book may be reproduced or transmitted in any form or by any means,
electronic or mechanical, including photocopying, recording, or by any
information storage and retrieval system, without written permission from the
publisher. For information, address Disney Press,
1200 Grand Central Avenue, Glendale, California 91201.

Printed in the United States of America

First Paperback Edition, April 2022

First Hardcover Edition, April 2022

1 3 5 7 9 10 8 6 4 2

ISBN 978-1-368-06803-1 (Paperback), ISBN 978-1-368-06973-1 (Hardcover)

FAC-020093-22063

Library of Congress Control Number: 2021947002

Book design by Catalina Castro

Visit disneybooks.com

DISNEY

# The ARISTOKITTENS

# The Great Biscuit Bake-Off

## By Jennifer Castle

## Illustrated by Sydney Hanson

DISNEY PRESS

Los Angeles • New York

# Chapter 1

Toulouse looked up at the wide, empty canvas sitting on the easel in front of him. Then he closed his eyes and thought: *Which color should I start with?*

He tried to remember exactly what he'd seen on that morning a few months earlier when he'd woken up on a riverbank in the French countryside. Toulouse; his brother, Berlioz; his sister, Marie; and their mama, Duchess, had all been "catnapped" away from their home.

It had been confusing and scary at the time, but now Toulouse looked back on it as a great adventure. After all, they'd met their stepfather, Thomas O'Malley, that day . . . and it had been their first time ever outside of Paris.

Now it all started coming back to Toulouse: the tall, thick blades of emerald-green grass, the brown cattails waving in the breeze, and the deep blue water that sparkled with sunlight.

"Hmmm," Toulouse said to himself. "What color were the flowers on the lily pads? Were they orange or pink? Or maybe orange-pink?"

Toulouse was working on a painting for a new "City Versus Country"–themed art exhibit at the Purrfect Paw-tisserie, the hidden creature café he ran with

Marie and Berlioz. They'd opened just a month earlier, in the basement of a famous restaurant.

*Jingle.* The front door of the café had a bell that rang every time a new customer came in. That day, the Paw-tisserie was quite busy, with the bell jingling every few minutes. This time, a pair of skunks sashayed in from the alley and up to the pastry case. It was filled with a rainbow of colorful treats that appealed to every type of animal. The skunks ordered two half-black, half-white cupcakes from the French bulldog working behind the counter. This was the kittens' friend Pierre, who lived with his human family upstairs and had helped Toulouse and his littermates start the café.

Toulouse glanced at the other

customers filling the tables, and at his brother, Berlioz, who was finishing a song on the piano.

Next to the piano, a small hedgehog sat by himself, listening. "Can you play 'Curl Into a Ball and Roll'?" he asked Berlioz. "My mama used to sing that with me."

"I'm sorry, Spike," Berlioz replied. "I don't know that one, but here's a little something I came up with the other day when I was trying to catch my own tail."

Berlioz began to play again, and the hedgehog happily bobbed his head to the beat as he took another bite of earthworm mousse.

The thought of earthworms reminded Toulouse again of the French countryside and that riverbank. *Aha!*

He finally remembered the color of the water lilies. He dipped his paw in the pink paint.

"*Ooh la la!*" someone squealed. "Marie, that looks so cute!"

The new sound made Toulouse lose his concentration. His beautiful flower ended up as a beautiful smudge.

Someone else let out a giggle. "Now *you* try! See if you can make a swirly design with the red icing."

Marie sat at a counter behind the pastry case. Next to her perched a white French bulldog puppy with three brown spots on her back. The puppy held a pastry bag, trying to squeeze red icing onto the top of a Bow-Wow Bonbon. It was one of Marie's specialties: a dog biscuit made with vanilla yogurt and

fresh berries in the shape of a giant
bone.

*Blurrrrrrp.*

Red icing squirted all over the dog
biscuit, the counter . . . and Marie's
whiskers.

Toulouse glared at them. He was the
painter. Why didn't they ask him for help
with the treat decorations?

"Oh, no!" the puppy cried, dropping
the decorating bag. "Marie, I'm so sorry!
I'm really bad at this!"

But Marie laughed. "It's okay,
Claudette. At least you decorated
*something*! Don't you think my fur looks
pretty this way?"

With one paw, Marie wiped some
icing off her longest whisker, stared at it,
and then flung it at Claudette. Giggling,

Claudette squeezed the tube and squirted some more at Marie.

"Knock it off!" Toulouse yowled at them, jumping down from his stool. "Nobody will want those messy treats."

"Oh, Toulouse," Marie said. "Don't be such a grump. I promised Claudette I'd teach her how to decorate pastries before her visit with her uncle Pierre was over. Her human family will be leaving Paris soon."

Marie put her paw on top of Claudette's.

"I'm going to miss you terribly, Claudette," Marie said. "It's been so much fun having you around here."

Toulouse flattened his ears as he glanced at the tray of Bow-Wow Bonbons. "How come you've never taught *me* to decorate your treats?"

Marie laughed. "You've never liked baking, Toulouse. Besides, your job at the café is to be the artist."

Toulouse looked sadly at his canvas. "I guess you're right. I do have a lot of artsy things to do around here. But . . ."

He took a deep breath, gathering the courage to tell Marie he really *did* want to learn to bake and decorate. But she and Claudette had gone back to the treats, giggling about how funny they looked. So he wiped his paw clean on a rag and went over to the piano, where Berlioz was playing the final notes of his song.

Spike, the hedgehog, clapped his tiny paws together. "Bravo! Bravo!"

"Thanks," Berlioz said to him, then turned to Toulouse. "Uh-oh. I know that look. It's your I'm-mad-at-Marie look."

Toulouse glanced back at Marie and Claudette, who were leaning in close to each other, smiling and whispering. "It's just strange to see our sister having so much fun with someone who's . . ."

"Not us?" Berlioz suggested.

Toulouse's ears and tail drooped. "I

thought *we* were her best friends. And why is Marie letting Claudette decorate the Bow-Wow Bonbons? She's not a chef."

"Maybe she doesn't want to take us away from our art and music," Berlioz replied. "Besides, you don't even like baking."

"Why does everyone keep saying that?" Toulouse said. "I've never tried it, but I'd like to. It looks fun."

Berlioz smiled, hopped down off his piano stool, and gave Toulouse a little boop on the nose with his paw.

"Don't be jealous," he said.

"I'm not jealous," Toulouse insisted, playfully swatting back at his brother.

"Oh, I don't know. I think if you were any more jealous, you'd go from being an orange cat to a *green* one. As in *green with envy*."

"You're going to get it for that!" Toulouse said, breaking into a mischievous smile.

"Just try!" Berlioz dared him, and took off running across the café. Toulouse started chasing. The two kittens raced around chairs and tables, accidentally bumping into a few of the legs. *Thump-thump-thump*.

Marie shook her head and sighed. "I apologize for my brothers!" she announced to all the customers. "It's a kitten thing."

Toulouse chased Berlioz toward the front door of the café and into a corner. "I've got you trapped!"

"*Mrow!*" Berlioz spat back, swiping at the air.

 12

Suddenly, the door to the café burst open.

*"AAAHHH-OOO!"*

Berlioz and Toulouse froze in fear, puffing up their fur.

A brown basset hound puppy with stubby legs and long, long ears stood in the doorway, howling at the top of his lungs.

*"AAAHHH-OOO!"* the basset hound howled a second time.

The café door opened again, and a chocolate-colored bloodhound puppy barreled in.

"Oh, shush, Leon," the bloodhound puppy said to the basset hound puppy. "You don't need to do that every time you walk into a place. Here, let me do it."

The bloodhound puppy sat down and planted her oversized paws firmly on the ground. "Attention, everyone at the Purrfect Paw-tisserie! We're looking for the three kittens who were catnapped from Paris by their evil butler! Are they here?"

The kittens exchanged nervous glances. Who were these strange puppies, and why were they looking for Berlioz, Marie, and Toulouse?

# Chapter 2

Toulouse and Berlioz raced across the
café and into the kitchen, then huddled
with their sister behind the pastry case.

Marie turned to their canine friend
Pierre. "Do you know those dogs?"

Pierre shook his head. "*Bah!* No. If I
did, I'm sure I'd remember that howl."

"One of us should find out what they
want," Berlioz said. "Marie, you're good
at that kind of thing."

Marie thought about it for a moment, swishing her tail. "That's true. I *am* a bit . . . gutsier than you two."

Toulouse bopped Marie on her ear. "Gutsy? I'll show you gutsy—"

"Hello?" The bloodhound puppy's voice echoed through the Paw-tisserie. "Three kittens? This is their café, isn't it?"

Before Marie could speak up, Toulouse summoned his courage, puffed up his fur, and stepped out in front of the pastry case.

"Hello," he said, trying to make his voice sound deeper. "I'm Toulouse, one of the kittens you're looking for. Can I help you?"

The puppy raised one eyebrow and stared at Toulouse with big dark eyes.

Toulouse stared back, not blinking. He swallowed hard. *Gulp.*

Then the puppy broke out into a toothy grin. "Leon, we found them!"

The two dogs bounded toward Toulouse in a flash of fur and wagging tails. The basset hound sniffed Toulouse's left ear, then the right. The bloodhound ruffled the fur on Toulouse's head with one big paw.

"We're mighty pleased to meet you," the bloodhound puppy told Toulouse. "I'm Nadine."

"Leon here," the basset hound announced, then carefully looked Toulouse up and down. "You're a *cat*. I've never gotten this close to a cat before."

"You smell funny," Nadine added.

"Hey, don't be rude," Leon scolded her, then turned back to Toulouse. "We've come a long way to meet you and the rest of your litter. All the way from the countryside, in fact."

Nadine took a look around the café, which had fallen silent since they'd walked in. All the animals were watching.

When Nadine spotted Toulouse's painting in the corner, she moved toward it. "Well, gosh-a-golly. That looks just like the riverbank where we live. And is that supposed to be a water lily?"

"Yes!" Toulouse replied. "You recognize all that?"

"Of course," Nadine replied. "That's where you and your family ended up the night you were catnapped. Right?"

"How did you know?" Toulouse asked with surprise.

Leon chimed in: "My dad, Lafayette, and Nadine's papa, Napoleon, found the basket you were sleeping in when the butler drove you into the country. Not too long after, we saw a newspaper that reported the story. We put two and two together."

"Don't you mean one and one?" Nadine asked.

"It's just an *expression*, smarty-paws," Leon said, rolling his eyes.

"*I'll* finish the story," Nadine announced. "So last month, we were out looking for scraps at a farm. . . . Early morning is the best time for that, because . . . Wait, that's not important. At the farm, we met some geese who'd just come back from Paris. They told us all about the catnapped kittens opening a creature café. Said it was the most special place they'd seen in the whole city!"

"We just had to meet you all and see it for ourselves," Leon added. "But where are the other kittens?"

"Hello!" Marie said as she marched out from behind the pastry case. "I'm

Marie. Welcome to the Purrfect Paw-tisserie."

After a moment, Berlioz crept out, too. "Hi, I'm Berlioz," he muttered.

"And I'm their friend Claudette," their puppy pal said as she joined the group.

Nadine looked at Toulouse, then Marie, then Berlioz. "So it's true? There's just three of you?"

"What happened to the rest of your litter?" Leon added.

"Leon!" Nadine exclaimed. "Remember, our papas told us to mind our manners when we got to Paris."

Toulouse puffed up his chest again. "We've always been a litter of three."

"Wow," Leon said, then paused to

scratch behind one ear with a hind leg. "I'm the oldest of *ten*."

"Me too," Nadine added proudly.

Claudette nodded. "That's the way it is with some puppies. My litter was five, but we all got adopted by different families."

"Only five?" Leon echoed. "And now you're alone?"

When Marie saw the hurt look on Claudette's face, she said, "Right now we're all together! If you've come all the way from the countryside, we should make it worth the trip. Have a seat and we'll bring you a tray of treats!"

The kittens took the dogs to the biggest table in the café, the blue one in the sunny corner.

Nadine and Leon hung back, circling Claudette and trying to sniff her.

"So . . . you live with a human family?" Leon asked her. "Doesn't that get boring?"

"I love my family," Claudette said. "And I never get bored. They take me everywhere! They have a big car and let me hang my head out the window."

"That's my favorite part, too," Leon said. "I've ridden in so many cars. Trucks, too! And wagons. And carriages."

"Madame has a carriage," Toulouse chimed in. "They're bumpy, but fun."

"And our friend Frou Frou the horse lets me ride on her hat," Berlioz added.

"Can't be as much fun as the sidecar

of a motorcycle," Nadine said. "That was the best thing ever."

Leon nodded. "We're really good at sneaking onto human moving machines without anyone seeing."

"We did that once!" Toulouse said. "When we were catnapped."

"Then you know how exciting it is," Nadine said with a sneaky smile. Then she turned to Claudette and asked, "Hey, how many human thingamajigs have you chewed up? I've ruined three pairs of slippers, a boot, a suitcase, an old umbrella . . ."

"I destroyed a *huuuuuuge* rubber ball!" Leon exclaimed.

Claudette looked down at the floor. "I don't chew up human things. That's naughty."

Nadine raised one eyebrow and glanced at Leon. Leon did the same thing back to Nadine.

"But I, um, do other cool things," Claudette offered, perking up her ears. "I can smell a stick of salami from the other side of the house!"

Nadine's eyes widened. "Wow, is that it? I have quite the sniffing record. I *am* a bloodhound, after all."

Marie glared at Nadine for a moment before announcing, "Claudette? Boys? I need to talk to you about a really important, um, problem with the, uh, oven."

She pulled Claudette, Berlioz, and Toulouse into a huddle on the other side of the café.

"Those puppies are really rude," Marie whispered.

"They're just being competitive," Toulouse said. "Maybe because they have so many brothers and sisters, they're always trying to feel special."

"But they're making *us* feel *bad*," Claudette added. "Whatever anyone says, they'll just come back with some way they're better."

"It is kind of annoying," Berlioz agreed, "even if they don't mean to be."

"It does seem like they turn everything into a contest," Toulouse said. "But what's so bad about that? Contests are fun."

"Hmmm," Marie said, her eyes lighting up with an idea. "You know what? If they want a contest, we can give them a contest. I'll be right back."

With that, she scampered off to the kitchen.

Fifteen minutes later, everyone in the café had gathered around two tables. Claudette sat at one, while Nadine and Leon sat at another.

Pierre and Marie emerged from the kitchen, pushing a tray that carried two identical large dog biscuits. They were shaped like hearts and decorated with red and green stripes.

"These biscuits are a new secret recipe I've been working on," Marie said. "I haven't told anybody what's in them. Not even my brothers!"

Toulouse frowned at Marie. "You're keeping a secret recipe from us?"

"I'm sure she'll tell us later," Berlioz whispered.

Marie turned to the crowd and announced, "There are six ingredients. Your challenge is to sniff out all of them."

"Easy as pie," Nadine said with a confident smile.

"You mean basic as a biscuit!" Leon said, nudging her.

They both laughed, then started examining the dog biscuit . . . with their noses. They sniffed the top; they sniffed the bottom. They sniffed all around the edges. Then they started whispering to each other.

"I like their strategy," Toulouse murmured to his sister.

At the other table, Claudette sat quietly, staring at her treat for a few moments. Then she took a long breath in through her nose, closing her eyes. She breathed out, then in again.

"I like *her* strategy better," Marie commented.

"Can we go first?" Nadine asked after a minute, excitedly hopping up and down on the chair.

Marie opened her mouth to reply, but Nadine didn't wait for an answer.

"Peanuts!" she announced. "Also cranberries! Honey, too . . ."

"Oats!" Leon exclaimed. "And flour . . . and . . ." He paused, stuck, then sniffed the treat again.

"Come on, Leon," Nadine said. "It must be whatever is making the green

color. Reminds me of home, actually. I think it must be . . ."

"Grass!" Leon declared.

"Yes, I think so, too." Nadine turned to Marie. "And grass. That's six. Did we guess them all?"

Marie slowly shook her head. "You got five, but one wasn't exactly right." Marie then turned to Claudette. "What do you think, Claudette?"

"I agree about the cranberries, honey, and oats," Claudette said slowly. "Peanut butter and flour, too."

Marie nodded. "Those five are correct. What about the sixth ingredient?"

Claudette took one last, long whiff of the biscuit.

"Do you know?" Nadine asked.

As Claudette paused, every animal in the café seemed to hold their breath, waiting for the answer. It was so quiet you could hear a mouse tiptoe.

"I think I do," Claudette said.

# Chapter 3

All eyes were on Claudette.

The little brown-spotted puppy sat up as tall as she could and thumped her tail twice against the chair.

"Spinach," she finally said. "I know that smell from the vegetable garden my humans keep."

Now everyone turned to Marie . . . who broke into a big smile and started purring loudly.

"You're right, Claudette!" she exclaimed. "It *is* spinach!"

All the animals in the café cheered, except for Nadine and Leon.

Toulouse went over to them. "You were close! Personally, I like grass better than spinach. . . ."

"That wasn't a fair contest," Leon muttered. "I bet Marie told Claudette her secret recipe."

Marie spun around to face them. "I would never, *ever* do that," she said, so insulted that the fur on her tail stood on end.

"Don't pay attention to him," Nadine told Marie. "He's just a sore loser. Nice job, Claudette."

"Thanks," Claudette replied.

Nadine added, "I've never even tasted spinach, let alone smelled it. Is that biscuit yummy?"

"If Marie made it, I'm sure it is!" Claudette said, then pointed toward the biscuits with her nose. "See for yourself!"

Nadine took a bite of the biscuit. Then Leon took a turn. They both chewed and crunched and slobbered.

"Well?" Marie asked.

"It's . . . kind of . . ." Leon began. *"Eh."*

Berlioz frowned. *"Eh?"*

"I agree," Nadine added. "It's . . . fine." She took another bite, then turned to Leon. "I bet we could make something that tasted even better."

"I bet you're right!" Leon replied. "We're puppies, not kittens, so we know dog biscuits. Imagine what we could create if we were back home in the countryside, where there are so many delicious ingredients to scavenge. Much more than in a city!"

Marie twitched her nose. "I disagree. Paris is full of different foods and flavors."

"It's true," Claudette added. "You

can find anything here if you know where to look."

"Do you think you could invent a better dog biscuit recipe than we could?" Nadine asked, tilting her head.

"No!" Claudette replied. "I was just—"

"Sure she could," Marie said. "I've been teaching her, and she's great at baking!"

"Oh, no," Berlioz groaned. "Not another argument."

Toulouse looked at the red-and-green heart-shaped biscuits, thinking about how he would have made them a different shape. Maybe a paw print, or a bumblebee to reflect the honey flavor. He knew if he had the chance, he could turn a dog treat into a work of art.

Suddenly, he had a brainstorm and motioned to Berlioz to step away from the group.

"Maybe another competition would be a good thing," Toulouse told his brother. "If the country puppies and Claudette want to see who can make the yummiest treat, we could make it an official contest. Everyone could taste the treats and vote on who should win."

Berlioz hesitated, looking over at the three puppies. Claudette had gone into the kitchen to wipe off her paws while Nadine and Leon were examining everything in the pastry case, trying to sniff through the glass.

Finally, Berlioz nodded. "Actually, I like that idea. If we really spread the word, I bet we'd get a lot of new customers to come to the café."

"Yes, you're right!" Toulouse agreed. "Let's tell Marie."

They called their sister over and filled her in. As they explained, her eyes lit up.

"What a wonderful idea!" she said.

"What should we call it?" asked Berlioz. "Every contest needs a catchy name. And a great prize, too!" Then his eyes lit up. "Oooh! I've got it! Our contest can be the Dog Biscuit Bake-Off."

"I like the sound of that!" Marie said.

"Me too," Toulouse agreed. "I didn't know you had these kinds of ideas in you, Berlioz."

Berlioz smiled shyly.

"What if the winner got their dog biscuit added to the Purrfect Paw-tisserie menu?" Toulouse added.

"Good thinking, Toulouse!" Berlioz said.

Toulouse scrambled to the top of the piano, with Marie following close behind. Berlioz pounced on the piano keys to get everyone's attention.

"Attention! Attention, everyone!" Toulouse announced. "We've decided to hold a Dog Biscuit Bake-Off! Anyone can enter, and anyone can come to taste and vote on their favorite. Whichever biscuit gets the most votes will be added to the Purrfect Paw-tisserie menu!"

"We're in!" Nadine and Leon shouted at the same time.

Claudette raised a paw. "I'll enter."

"Anyone else?" Toulouse offered. Not a peep, squeak, honk, quack, bark, or meow. "Well, think about it. All you have to do is bring your treat here in two days, at noon, for judging."

The café was suddenly abuzz with excitement about the contest. Marie and Toulouse leapt down from the piano, and Claudette padded over.

"What did I just sign up for?" Claudette asked Marie. "I'm not sure I can actually create a treat recipe."

"Don't worry. I'll help you," Marie said to her friend.

"I can help, too," Toulouse offered.

Marie glanced at Claudette, then back at her brother. "Oh . . . er . . . I was thinking this could just be a girl thing for

Claudette and me. I don't think you'd have any fun."

A hurt look flashed across Toulouse's face, but he quickly tried to hide it. "Yeah, sure. I probably wouldn't."

Marie turned away and began whispering to Claudette. Berlioz started playing one of his jazz tunes while a crowd of animals gathered around to watch and dance.

Then Toulouse spied his painting in the corner. It was still sitting unfinished on the easel, with that big pink smudge that was supposed to be a flower.

"I must be good for something else around here," he muttered to himself.

He heard Nadine and Leon bickering behind him.

"I like your ideas for ingredients,"

Nadine said. "But where will we find them here in Paris?"

"And you have a great plan for the decorations," Leon added. "But we're not exactly artists."

Toulouse's ears perked up, and he slowly approached the puppies.

"Ahem . . ." he said, his whiskers twitching nervously. "I think I can help you with both of those problems."

"What do you mean?" Nadine asked.

Toulouse took a deep breath, then smiled. "Let me join your Dog Biscuit Bake-Off team and you'll find out."

# Chapter 4

Two brown puppies chased an orange
kitten down a Paris sidewalk, weaving in
and out of the afternoon bustle of cars,
wagons, and horse-drawn carriages.

At least, that was what it looked like.
But the dogs weren't chasing the cat.
Toulouse was leading his new friends to
his third most favorite place in the city:
the Luxembourg Gardens.

(His first favorite place was home, of
course, and second was the Paw-tisserie.)

"Whenever I need inspiration for a painting, I come here!" Toulouse called to Nadine and Leon. "Being outside helps me think, so maybe it'll help us brainstorm for the Bake-Off."

The puppies caught up with Toulouse as they rounded the corner into the park. It was a typical day at the Luxembourg Gardens: people walking in pairs or groups or sitting on blankets in the sun. A woman pushed a baby carriage past them.

Leon shook his head, his long basset hound ears brushing the ground. "I'll never understand why humans can't carry their young in their mouths, like dogs and cats do. They must be so lazy."

Toulouse laughed. "I've never thought of it that way! There's a lot I don't understand about humans, but at least they're interesting. Come on. There's so much I want to show you."

He started running along the path, but when he looked back, Nadine and Leon were no longer right behind him. Instead, they'd raced off in another direction, yipping with excitement.

"Hey, guys!" Toulouse shouted. "My mama says you're supposed to stay on the—"

The puppies, headed straight for a thicket of bushes that was separated from the path by a little fence, were too far away to hear him. Toulouse had often seen those bushes and wandered over to investigate, but he had always been too nervous to go past the fence.

"It's okay to explore a bit, darling," his mama, Duchess, always said. "But be careful and listen to your whiskers: they'll tell you if something's not safe."

Now Nadine was jumping over the fence and Leon was crawling under it.

When he reached the other side, Leon called, "Here, kitty, kitty! Are you coming or not?"

Toulouse stood very still for a moment. His whiskers seemed to be saying, *You'll be fine as long as you stay with the puppies.* He took a deep breath and ran under the fence as fast as he could. He followed Nadine and Leon into the bushes. There, it was cool and dark, like a little secret cave.

"You're right, Toulouse," Nadine

said. "The park *is* fun. Show us the best hiding spots in here."

"H-h-hiding spots?" Toulouse stammered.

"Yes. Where do you go when you want to jump out suddenly and bark at something?" Leon asked. "Or, I mean, *meow*?"

"I don't usually—"

"We're here to get inspiration for the Bake-Off, remember?" Nadine reminded Leon.

"You and Toulouse can work on that part," Leon said to Nadine, giving her a little kick with a back leg. "You're better at that brainstorming stuff anyway. I'm the chaser and fetcher."

Toulouse tilted his head. "That sounds like me and my brother and sister.

We each have something we're really good at."

"Yup," Nadine said. "Leon's been teaching me how to run faster, and I show him how to calm down enough to do some thinking."

"Really?" Toulouse asked with surprise. "You don't just stick to your own jobs?"

Leon exclaimed, "Of course not! It would be boring to do only one thing all the time." He spotted a branch above his head, then reached out and grabbed it with both paws. "You have to *branch out*, get it?"

"We both wanted to get better at finding hiding spots," Nadine told Toulouse, "so we took lessons from our dads."

"Should we give you some tips?" Leon asked, and Toulouse nodded. "Well, first you get as low as you can to the ground. Then you keep climbing over roots and under branches. . . ."

"Go as far as you can into the bushes," Nadine continued, "until you find a place where the leaves are so thick nobody would ever see you in there. But also not so thick that you can't see out. Then, you watch."

"Like this," Leon said, and motioned for Toulouse and Nadine to follow him farther into the web of branches. They scrambled over some and scooted under others, their bellies almost touching the ground.

Finally, Leon stopped in what seemed like the deepest spot inside the thicket. "This is the perfect spot. Gather in close."

They huddled together in the space, which was just big enough for the three of them. The wall of leaves had a tiny gap in the middle, like a window for them to peek out.

"Pretty cool, eh?" Nadine said, nudging Toulouse.

Toulouse breathed deep and took it all in. The smell of dirt and greenery whirled around him, and the air felt heavier. People in the park were going about their business, with no idea that there were two puppies and a kitten watching them from a secret hideaway.

"*Super* cool," Toulouse said with a sigh. "I wish I could come here and paint."

"Hey, let's be quiet for a few seconds," Nadine whispered. "This is a good thinking place."

After just a moment of silence, Leon said impatiently, "I don't hear any ideas, but I do hear a wagon coming."

"How can you tell it's a wagon?" Toulouse asked.

Nadine and Leon explained what to listen for: the way the wheels squeaked, how fast they squeaked, and the kind of noise they made on the dirt of the park path.

"I've never been good at reading sounds that way," Toulouse said. "But I'm *great* at reading colors and shapes."

"What do you mean?" Leon asked, frowning.

Toulouse pointed with his paw to a woman sitting on a nearby bench, reading a book.

"See her dress?" Toulouse asked. "It's dark blue. That's a serious color. And the curve of her back as she's bending over the book, like she wants to dive into the pages? It's human body-speak for *I'm thinking hard*. So I bet she's sad about something."

Leon and Nadine both stared at Toulouse, their puppy noses twitching.

"I know, it sounds weird," Toulouse admitted, pawing at the dirt with his front claws. "Berlioz and Marie are always making fun of me for stuff like that."

"No!" Nadine said. "It's not weird at all. It's neat that you know so much about colors and shapes. That'll really help us make a treat that will win the Bake-Off!"

Toulouse smiled with surprise. "Thanks! So . . . what else do you country puppies like to do outdoors?"

Nadine and Leon exchanged glances.

"It rained last night," Nadine said to Leon.

"I was thinking the same thing," Leon said back.

"MUD BATH!" they both exclaimed.

"Follow us," Nadine said to Toulouse. After they squirmed out of their hiding bush, all three friends took off across a lawn of green grass toward an area filled with tall trees. Nadine and Leon kept their noses close to the ground, sniffing for something.

"Found some!" Leon shouted, then threw himself into a muddy patch. After rolling back and forth a few times, he stood up and shook the mud off his fur. It surrounded him like a gray cloud.

"Too dusty," he declared. "We're

looking for wet mud—the kind that feels cold and soft on your fur and gets you really messy."

"Like this," Nadine said, sniffing at the base of another tree. She threw herself onto the ground and came back up covered in drippy brown stuff. "It's the best."

Leon bounded over and did the same. "Woo-hoo!"

"Getting dirty for fun isn't really a cat thing . . ." Toulouse murmured, but the puppies didn't hear him. Then Toulouse spotted something: some of the mud had splattered onto the tree trunk in an interesting shape. It reminded him of deer antlers.

Toulouse dipped his paw in the mud and drew a head underneath the antlers.

Another dip into the mud and he added
a body, then legs. He stepped back to
admire his work.

Leon looked at the tree trunk and
stopped his mud roll. "Wow!"

"Toulouse, let's give your deer a
name," Nadine added.

"Wait, you can tell it's a deer?" Toulouse asked them.

"Of course!" Leon said, laughing. "It looks just like the one on the sign at an inn near our home. Every night we howl outside the door and the chef gives us leftovers."

"Berlioz and Marie can never tell what I'm painting," Toulouse said, shaking his head in amazement. "But you do."

"Hey, let's pretend we're chasing that deer right now!" said Nadine.

Nadine, Leon, and Toulouse took off together through the trees, with the puppies spraying mud as they went. They scampered across another field, around a flower garden, and up a flight of stone steps, laughing the whole way.

"This is the most fun I've had in the park *ever*!" Toulouse shouted to his new friends.

And then . . .

*WHOMP!*

He ran right into something big and furry.

Toulouse stumbled backward. When he looked up, he was staring right into the eyes of an orange-and-white cat—a very *familiar* one. The cat was thumping his tail on the ground.

It was Toulouse's stepdad, Thomas O'Malley.

"Well, hey now," Thomas said. "If it isn't the kitten I've been sent to find because he's late for dinner."

"I'm so sorry . . ." Toulouse muttered. "I, uh, lost track of time."

Nadine and Leon had skidded to a stop at the sight of the big alley cat. "We were working on our Dog Biscuit Bake-Off idea," Nadine said.

Thomas O'Malley looked over the three mud-covered critters and broke into a sly grin. "If your dog biscuit is going to be made of mud, it certainly looks like you were working pretty hard."

Toulouse turned to the puppies. "I have to go, but come by my house tomorrow. Just ask any dog you see where Madame Adelaide Bonfamille and her cats live, and they'll show you the way."

"Can't wait!" Leon said. "Our treat's going to be so yummy."

"Better than yummy," Nadine

added. "Toulouse, with your help, it's going to *win*."

Toulouse waved goodbye and followed Thomas O'Malley out of the park, smiling all the way home.

# Chapter 5

It was Monday, which meant the Purrfect Paw-tisserie was closed and the kittens had the day off to play at home. Marie had gone out to meet Claudette, leaving Toulouse and Berlioz to come up with a two-cat game.

*Thwap.*

Berlioz batted a red pom-pom down the long downstairs hallway. It rolled and rolled and rolled . . .

Until Toulouse sprang out, in a

flash of orange fur, from a doorway. He caught the pom-pom with one paw.

"Good pounce!" Berlioz said. "My turn. Hit it back to me."

As Toulouse knocked the pom-pom toward his brother, he said, "Berlioz, um . . . I have something to tell you."

Berlioz jumped on the pom-pom with both paws and grabbed it in his mouth. "Zhat shounds sherious."

"I'm, uh, helping Nadine and Leon with their entry for the Bake-Off," Toulouse said.

The pom-pom plopped out of Berlioz's mouth. "So you really are interested in baking?"

"Yes, I really am. After all, I love eating treats. So I'd like to learn how to make and decorate treats, too, you know?" Toulouse sat down and laid his head sadly on his paws. "It seems like Marie only cares about Claudette these days, and she doesn't think I'd be any good at baking or decorating. But I want to prove to her that I can do it."

"Let me guess," Berlioz said, abandoning the pom-pom to join his brother. "Nadine and Leon *do* think you'd be good at baking and decorating?"

"Yes," Toulouse said. "Also, they're really fun. If you and Marie got to know them, I bet you'd like them, too."

Berlioz thought for a moment. "I'm glad you're trying something new."

"Hey, Berlioz! Why don't you join our team?"

"Thanks for the invitation, but no, I'm busy," Berlioz said. "Speaking of trying something new, I had a great idea about how to get more people to come to the Bake-Off, so I'm—"

Suddenly, Duchess's voice echoed down the hallway. "Toulouse! Toulouse? Are you back here?"

"Yes, Mama!" Toulouse replied.

Duchess rounded the corner and smiled when she saw her kittens.

"Darling, you have visitors," she

said to Toulouse. "Two puppies named Nadine and Leon, I believe? They seem very nice, even if they did forget to say *please* when they asked to see you."

"Those are my new friends. Thank you, Mama!" Toulouse turned to his brother. "Looks like my Bake-Off team needs me, but we can finish talking when I get home."

Berlioz's tail dropped. "Sure."

Toulouse dashed off down the hallway, toward the front hall. He found Nadine and Leon sniffing their way along the tiled floor.

"Hi!" Toulouse greeted them.

"Fancy house," Nadine commented.

"With a lot of fancy smells," Leon added.

"We did some more thinking at the

park," Nadine told Toulouse, "and we came up with the best dog biscuit recipe. With your amazing decorations, it'll win, for sure."

"We're calling it Country Days Delight," Leon explained. "It's made up of all the yummy foods they give us at that inn near our home. The deer you painted with mud was the inspiration for the recipe!"

"But for this contest, we have to get ingredients the hard way," Nadine said. "Toulouse, can you help us find them?"

Toulouse's face lit up. "Of course! What do you need?"

The best food market in Paris was ten blocks from Madame's house: six blocks toward the midday sun, then four blocks toward the Eiffel Tower. Toulouse's mission was to get a sweet potato, which was hard to find, but he knew just the right market stand. He pranced down the street, feeling proud that his new friends had given him such an important job.

At the end of the second block, he was about to step off the curb and cross the street when—*KA-RUMP.*

Something white and furry landed on top of him. Toulouse tried to kick it away with his back paws but stopped when he saw that the something wore a pink ribbon around its neck.

*"Marie?"*

"I could smell you coming from around the corner!" Marie said, laughing. "I don't think there are any other cats in Paris who smell like oil paint, fish, *and* fresh cream."

"What are you doing here?" Toulouse asked. "I thought you were at the café, working on your Bake-Off recipe with Claudette."

"I was," Marie replied. "But we need one more ingredient, and there's only one place I've ever seen them in the city."

They both narrowed their eyes in suspicion.

"*Sweet potato?*" they asked at the same time.

"Why do *you* need a sweet potato?" Marie asked Toulouse.

"It's . . . um . . . for Nadine and Leon's recipe."

The fur on Marie's tail puffed up a bit. "You're helping them?"

Toulouse pushed out his chin. "Yes."

"But why?"

"Because I have some great ideas. You and Claudette didn't want anyone else on your team, but Nadine and Leon did. They wanted *me*."

Marie rolled her eyes. "Oh, Toulouse. You're great at art, but baking and cooking aren't exactly your thing."

Toulouse stared at her. "I can have more than one *thing*, you know. I'll show you how good I am at finding ingredients!"

Then he suddenly launched himself over the curb and headed for the next street.

"Oh, no you don't!" Marie called from behind him. "I'm going to get to that market first!"

Toulouse raced along the sidewalk, with Marie right behind him. She was close enough that she kept batting at Toulouse's tail as they ran. The sidewalk was like a big obstacle course, and the kittens weaved through human legs, baby carriage wheels, and dogs on leashes.

After two blocks, Toulouse hit a bumpy patch of cobblestones and stumbled. Marie caught up and leapt onto his back.

"Gotcha . . . again!" she said. Before Toulouse could react, she hopped off him and started running. Now it was Toulouse's turn to chase his sister.

Marie rounded the corner toward the market and tried to scramble around

a man pushing a cart. Toulouse caught up and swatted at her tail.

"Now we're even!" he cried, and kept racing down the street. Marie followed, and within a few seconds, they were running alongside each other.

Their finish line was up ahead: a market stand with a big sign reading BELLE JOUR FARMS. The stand was crowded with baskets full of all types of vegetables: green lettuce, red onions, yellow peppers, purple eggplants.

A huge fluffy gray dog lay stretched out on the ground under the stand.

Marie got to him first and caught her breath. "Hello, monsieur! Do you remember us? We usually come here with our friend Pierre."

The dog lifted his head and peered

at Marie and Toulouse. "Ah, yes. From the Purrfect Paw-tisserie?"

The kittens nodded, still huffing and puffing from their chase.

The dog gave them a sideways glance. "I have to say, I've never seen anyone—human or animal—so eager to buy vegetables."

"We need just one today," Marie said.

"Actually, two," Toulouse said, correcting her.

The dog slowly stood up, stretching his front legs, then his back legs. Toulouse and Marie flicked their tails impatiently.

"All right, then," he said. "What can I get you *two* of?"

"Sweet potatoes!" Marie and Toulouse said.

The dog frowned, then shook his head. "I'm sorry, but we've been very busy today and sold the last sweet potato a few minutes ago. We'll have some more tomorrow, though. Come back in the morning."

He flopped back down on the ground and closed his eyes.

Disappointed and frustrated, Toulouse and Marie walked slowly toward home. After several blocks of awkward silence, Marie finally turned to her brother.

"So," she said, "have you tasted Nadine and Leon's treat recipe?"

"Not yet," Toulouse admitted. "But it's going to be delicious. It'll definitely *look* delicious with the decorations I'm planning."

Marie flattened her ears. "Mine and Claudette's, too."

"I guess we'll just have to wait and see which one the customers like more," Toulouse said.

They were quiet for a few awkward moments as they turned up the path to the front door of Madame Adelaide's mansion.

Finally, Marie mumbled, "I guess you were serious about wanting to help me with my baking."

"Of course I was," Toulouse said. "I thought it would be fun to try something new. You probably wouldn't understand."

"But I do!" Marie protested. "I don't

want to just be baking and cooking all the time, either. I would love to—"

Before she could finish, a horse trotted by, pulling a carriage. The wheels sprayed water into the air, and Marie jumped to avoid it. She landed in front of Toulouse. The two kittens just stared at each other, not sure what to say next.

"Guess what?" Toulouse said.

"What?" Marie asked.

"Last one through the cat door is a sticky-paw!"

Toulouse started running.

"Hey!" Marie called, chasing after him. They had just about reached the door at the same time when Berlioz's head popped through from inside.

*"Aaaah!"* Berlioz said, then gave a

little hiss as he pushed his way out. "You scared me!"

"Sorry," Marie said.

"Also, sorry I was gone so long, Berlioz," Toulouse added. "Do you want to finish our game?"

"Maybe later," Berlioz said, running off down the path to the street. "Can't talk now! I'm in a rush!"

Toulouse and Marie watched their brother disappear around a corner.

"Why was he in such a hurry?" Marie asked.

Toulouse thought for a moment, flicking his tail up and down. "Hmmm. Earlier, he was about to tell me about a great new idea he has for the café. Maybe it has something to do with that."

Marie narrowed her eyes. "*Hmmm* is right."

All they could do now was wait and see how the Bake-Off would play out the next day—and maybe Berlioz's big idea would be revealed then, too.

# Chapter 6

DOG BISCUIT BAKE-OFF TODAY

TAKE A NIBBLE AND CAST YOUR VOTE

**T**oulouse stepped back from the banner to wipe his paws clean of blue paint and admire his work. Soon the Paw-tisserie would open its doors and lots of customers would arrive. Berlioz had been running around all morning, spreading news about the Bake-Off among the animals of Paris.

Toulouse hoped all those customers would think that the Country Days Delight was the tastiest treat. He had managed to find that sweet potato and the other ingredients in Nadine and Leon's recipe. Then he'd had the idea that the puppies should bake the treats in a pie shape so they could serve them as slices. Toulouse used icing to draw a little red deer on each treat, beaming proudly at how they turned out.

Marie and Claudette emerged from the kitchen area, whispering to each other. They stopped when they spotted Toulouse.

"Look, it's my brother," Marie declared. "A member of the losing Bake-Off team."

Toulouse rolled his eyes and replied,

"And hi to my sister, who'll definitely win the award for Most Annoying."

"I'm not overconfident," Marie protested. "I'm just telling the truth."

"The Bake-Off hasn't even happened yet, and the truth might surprise you."

Marie stared at her brother. "I really wish I could pounce on you right now. But I'm a lady, and ladies don't tussle in cafés. Especially ones that they run."

"Lucky for us both, huh?" Toulouse said.

He walked away, his tail swishing back and forth behind him.

A short time later, the café officially opened for the contest. Berlioz had apparently done a great job spreading the word, because it was quickly crowded with customers eager to taste and vote in the Dog Biscuit Bake-Off.

Pierre and Toulouse had arranged the tables to display the entries. Leon and Nadine's biscuits were in a big flat basket, while Claudette's biscuits sat on a fancy round plate decorated with fruit. Her treats were covered in yellow icing and shaped like bananas. The

sign behind the plate read TROPICAL
ADVENTURE TREATS.

Pierre stood with Duchess and
Thomas O'Malley, examining the two
entries.

"I have to say, I'm impressed with
these puppies," Pierre said.

"Don't forget the kittens who
helped them," Duchess added, flashing
a smile at Thomas. She turned to Marie
and Toulouse. "I'm so proud of you,

Toulouse, for trying something different!
And you, too, Marie, for working so
well with a new friend. As for
Berlioz . . ."

Duchess looked around.

"Berlioz? Where are you, darling?"

"He must still be out on the streets,
spreading the word about the Bake-Off,"
Toulouse suggested.

Suddenly, Berlioz rushed in from
outside. "I'm here! I'm here! I'm so sorry
I'm late! Has the tasting started yet?"

"You're just in time," Toulouse
replied. "Which do you think looks
better? The Country Days Delight or the
Tropical Adventure Treats?"

"They, er, both look yummy," Berlioz
muttered, then made a beeline for the
piano. He sat down and started playing

a bouncy jazz tune that made the café seem extra festive.

Toulouse turned to Marie. "Does Berlioz seem odd to you?"

Marie nodded. "Yes, but we can talk to him about it later. It's time to start the judging. I'm going to get up on the piano and make an announcement—"

Toulouse stepped in front of her. "Why do *you* always make the announcements?"

"Because I have the loudest voice," Marie said.

"Don't be so sure."

He opened his mouth and started to yowl.

"Toulouse! Haven't I taught you that yowling indoors is rude?" Duchess said.

Toulouse stopped yowling and shut his mouth. "Sorry, Mama."

Duchess turned to Pierre. "I believe this is more of a barking occasion. Would you do the honors?"

"My pleasure," Pierre said before he let out a loud *woof*! And then another. Then a few more.

Every creature in the Purrfect Paw-tisserie fell silent.

"Welcome to our first ever Dog Biscuit Bake-Off!" Pierre called. "Everyone, please take just one sample of the Country Days Delight and one sample of the Tropical Adventure Treats. Then decide for yourself which one you like better."

"Hi! Hello, hello! Pierre?" someone

with a high, squeaky voice piped up. It was Pouf, the squirrel. "What about the third treat?"

"Pardon me?" Pierre asked.

"The third treat! On the table with the other two! It's right here and it looks really delicious and I can't wait to try it, actually I think I'll taste that one first—"

*"Bah!"* Pierre exclaimed. "There's a third entry?"

Marie and Toulouse looked at each other. *A third entry?*

Both kittens scrambled over to the judging table. Sure enough, in addition to Claudette's plate and Nadine and Leon's basket, there was a tray covered in leaves and blades of grass, and it was filled with little oval treats frosted in bright colors: pink, yellow, green. The name Eggs-ellent Eats was written on a leaf that was fastened to a stick in the middle of the tray.

Marie leaned over and sniffed.

"Hmmm," she said. "These smell sweet. Sugary and buttery."

Leon, Nadine, and Claudette also rushed to see.

"Wait," Nadine said. "Were you expecting a third treat?"

"Did anyone else say they were entering?" Leon asked.

"Not to me," Marie replied. "What about you, Toulouse?"

Toulouse shook his head. "Me neither. Is there a name on the entry?"

Leon, who'd been carefully inspecting the tray of treats, said, "No."

"Hey, everyone!" Nadine shouted to all the customers with a little bark. "Whose entry is this?"

They looked out at the other animals in the café. Which one was the mystery biscuit chef?

## Chapter 7

**N**obody spoke up or stepped forward.

"Um, these treats didn't bake themselves!" Leon said.

"It must be an anonymous entry," Toulouse said to Marie.

"Should that be allowed?" Marie asked.

"I don't know," Toulouse replied. "Let's ask Berlioz."

Toulouse and Marie pulled their

brother away from the piano and into a corner to discuss.

"It seems strange that someone would bring an entry and not put their name on it," Toulouse said. "I don't think we should let it be judged."

"Oh, Toulouse, you just don't want the extra competition," Marie scoffed. "But don't worry. Claudette's treat will win anyway."

"How can you be so sure?" Toulouse asked. "I just heard a poodle saying how much she loves the decorations on our treats."

Marie glared. "I can't believe you teamed up with Nadine and Leon. You've just met them!"

"Well, *they* didn't make fun of me when I said I wanted to learn to bake."

"Stop bickering, you two!" Berlioz said. "We're supposed to be talking about the Eggs-ellent Eats."

"Okay," Marie said. "What do *you* think, Berlioz?"

"I think it's okay that there's an anonymous entry in the Bake-Off," Berlioz replied. "And I also think it's okay if we want to do more than one thing at the Paw-tisserie. It was fun this morning when I went out to spread the word. I met a lot of interesting animals, and I have more ideas to help the café get new customers."

Marie looked away. "I never said we could only do one thing here. In fact, I've been wanting to help you with the entertainment, Berlioz. I would love to start singing again. I just thought both of you wanted to stick with what you know best!"

Berlioz and Toulouse stared at Marie with surprise. Before either of them could reply, Pierre stepped into the middle of the trio.

"So? What did you three decide?" Pierre asked.

Berlioz jumped onto the piano keys and announced in his loudest, most official-sounding voice, "The third entry is allowed! Let the tasting begin!"

There was a sudden buzz of barks, meows, squawks, squeaks, and other noises as all the animals started tasting the treats.

*"Mmmmmmmm-eow,"* Thomas O'Malley purred as he sampled the Country Days Delight.

"Scrump-de-li-icious!" Pouf, the squirrel, said, licking every last crumb of a Tropical Adventure Treat from his paws.

*"Grrrrrr-yummy,"* Pierre growled as he nibbled on an Eggs-ellent Eat.

"You'd better taste Claudette's treats before they're gone," Marie said to her brothers.

"You two try the Country Days Delight," Toulouse urged them.

The kittens took one of each biscuit. They shared a Country Days Delight and a Tropical Adventure Treat.

"Mmmmm," Toulouse and Marie both said at the same time.

"This really does remind me of a country inn," Marie said. "It's actually . . .

er . . . well, very delicious. And the pie-slice design is super creative."

Toulouse licked his lips. "This treat is definitely a tropical adventure. . . . Marie, it could be, uh, a great one to have on the menu."

Then Berlioz chimed in, holding up a half-eaten Eggs-ellent Eat. "Don't forget the last biscuit."

Toulouse took one, broke it in half, and gave the other half to Marie.

After a few nibbles, Toulouse said, "Wow. I taste the egg, but also fruit and vegetables. . . ."

"And something sweet," Marie said. "It all reminds me of a garden."

"These taste like springtime!" Toulouse added. "Are there actually flowers in this recipe?"

"Yes," Berlioz replied. "They're amazing, right?"

Toulouse frowned. "How would you know?"

Berlioz just smiled and returned to the piano to play.

Marie and Toulouse followed him, but before they could pester their brother with more questions, Pierre appeared and said, "*Bah!* Every last treat from all three entries has been gobbled up! It's time to take a vote."

He hopped up onto a chair and barked everyone to attention.

"Are you all ready to choose a winner of the Dog Biscuit Bake-Off?" he asked, and all the animals replied with a chorus of sounds.

"Who thinks the Country Days Delight should be the winner?"

Some of the animals piped up. Nadine and Leon looked very pleased with themselves.

"Who thinks the Tropical Adventure Treats should be the winner?" Pierre asked.

Other animals piped up this time. They sounded about as loud as the first group—there was no clear winner yet. Claudette reacted with a happy yip.

"And finally," Pierre continued, "who thinks the Eggs-ellent Eats deserve the title?"

This time, the noise was much louder and longer than it was for the first two. There was no question who'd received the most votes. Nadine, Leon, and Claudette all looked at one another with shock and disappointment.

"It sounds like we have a clear winner!" Pierre announced. "Will the creator of the Eggs-ellent Eats please come forward?"

The café fell silent. All the animals looked around, eager to see who the mystery biscuit baker was. After a few long moments, a high, faint squeak rose from the corner of the room.

"It was me," the little voice's owner said.

The crowd of animals parted as something made its way to the piano. It moved along the floor until it reached Berlioz's piano bench. Berlioz bent down and helped it climb up to the keyboard.

It was a hedgehog.

"*Spike?*" Toulouse asked, his eyes wide with surprise.

"Hello, all," Spike said, then shyly hung his head. "I'm so happy you liked my treats. Thank you." Spike then turned to Berlioz. "Thanks especially to you, Berlioz, for helping me find all the ingredients I needed."

"Berlioz . . . *helped you?*" Marie asked. Berlioz twitched his tail nervously.

"I . . . um . . . did. Spike told me he wanted to make up a treat recipe inspired by his favorite food, eggs, and his favorite season, spring. I thought it was a great idea and wanted to lend a paw! So I went into the park and asked every animal I saw what flavors and smells meant springtime to them, and we came up with the list of ingredients. I came up with the name Eggs-ellent Eats, too!"

"Why didn't you tell us that you and Spike were entering the Bake-Off?" Marie asked.

"You and Toulouse were already arguing about helping different teams, and I didn't want us all to be mad at one another." Berlioz turned to his brother. "Toulouse, remember when you said you entered the Bake-Off with Nadine and Leon because you wanted to try something new?"

Toulouse nodded.

"It was the same for me," Berlioz continued. "I can be more than just the musical kitten in the family. . . . I'd like to be other things, too—like someone who can run special events at the café and advertise them to all the animal customers out there."

All three kittens were quiet for a few moments, letting that sink in.

"You did a great job, Berlioz," Toulouse finally said.

Marie sighed. "And, Toulouse, your treats looked and tasted amazing."

Pierre cleared his throat and let out a soft bark. "It sounds just right to me that each Bake-Off entry had some help from one of the kittens. I'm pleased to officially announce Spike, the hedgehog, and his delicious Eggs-ellent Eats the winner of the Purrfect Paw-tisserie Dog Biscuit Bake-Off!"

The animals started to cheer again, but Spike frantically waved his little paws around.

"No, no, no!" he cried. "Please stop!"

# Chapter 8

The café fell silent.

"What do you mean, *stop*?" Nadine asked Spike.

"I don't want to be called the winner!" Spike replied.

"Who wouldn't want that?" Leon added.

"We're happy for you, Spike," Claudette said. "Your treats really were the best."

Spike smiled. "I'm glad everyone

liked them. But I didn't enter them to win or get them on the menu. That's why I didn't put my name on the entry. I baked them because it made me happy, and it made me even happier to see all my friends and neighbors eating them."

"So, wait," Nadine said. "You did all that work just for *fun*?"

Spike smiled big and puffed up his spines. "I did."

Toulouse turned to his littermates. "Marie, Berlioz, I have an idea! Spike just reminded me why we started the café in the first place: because we all love making things and sharing them. Nadine and Leon and Claudette, you feel the same way, right?"

"I do like winning," Leon said. "But . . . maybe that's not so important. I really liked sharing the biscuits we made with all of you, too."

"I agree," said Nadine. "And, uh . . . maybe we got a little *too* competitive and forgot that the treats are the best part. Claudette, your biscuit was super delicious."

Claudette smiled. "Thanks. I liked yours, too."

"What if . . ." Toulouse began, "we added all *three* biscuits to the menu?"

After a moment, Berlioz said, "I love it!"

Marie smiled. "I've been wanting to have more dog biscuits in the pastry case. And, Toulouse, if you can do some of the baking, I'll have more time to start singing again. If Berlioz is okay with that, of course."

"I'm okay with that!" Berlioz
said. "It'll free up some time for me to
promote the café."

"So it's a paws-up from you both?"
Toulouse asked eagerly.

"Paws up!" Marie said.

"Way up!" Berlioz added.

Toulouse gave Pierre a nod, and
Pierre got ready to make another
announcement.

"Everyone," Pierre barked, "we have
some exciting news!"

The next day, the three kittens and three puppies sat together in the alley outside the Purrfect Paw-tisserie.

Claudette hugged Marie. "I'm going to miss you so much."

"Me too," Marie replied. "Your humans come visit Pierre's humans every few months, right? So you'll have lots to tell me when you come back again."

Nadine and Leon wagged their tails.

"And we'll never forget how much fun we had on our Paris adventure," Leon said.

"We're so glad we met you!" Nadine added.

"Us too," Berlioz said.

"Would you all want to come visit us

in the country sometime?" Nadine asked. "You too, Claudette! We can go on a sniffing adventure together."

Claudette barked her approval.

"I would love that," Toulouse said. "I could bring my art supplies, and paint without having to guess what colors things are."

"So we won't all say goodbye," Marie said. "Just au revoir . . . until we see you again."

"Yes!" Claudette said, then booped Marie on the nose. "That'll be soon, I promise." She bounded up the alley and turned at the corner to meet up with her human family.

"See you soon, Monsieur Artiste," Leon said to Toulouse, playfully swatting him on the nose.

"Go find some great new hiding spots in the park for us," Nadine added.

"I will," Toulouse said. "But how are you two getting home?"

"Pierre told us where we can hop on the back of a truck headed to the countryside," Leon replied.

"I'll find one first!" Nadine cried, launching herself up the alley.

"Not unless I do!" Leon called, chasing after her.

The kittens watched them disappear around the corner, then turned to one another.

"So . . ." Marie said.

"It's just us again," Toulouse added.

"And a Paw-tisserie full of customers," Berlioz reminded them.

"Who'd have thought, just a short

time ago, that we'd be running a café together?" Marie wondered aloud. "We were so good at teamwork when we started the Paw-tisserie. Then we got all jealous and competitive. What happened?"

"I don't know," Toulouse replied, thinking hard. "I guess I saw you having fun with your baking, and I wanted to try, too. I felt really sad when you were teaching Claudette but not me."

"I'm sorry," Marie said. "I didn't mean to hurt your feelings."

"And, Toulouse, I get lots of ideas for promoting the café and for exciting events," Berlioz told his brother, "but that seemed like your thing, with your art shows and signs. I thought you'd get annoyed if I did that kind of stuff, too."

"Berlioz, that wouldn't annoy me . . . but someone keeping a secret from me does!" said Toulouse.

"Got it—no more secrets," Berlioz said, and the brothers smiled at each other.

Marie had been thinking hard. "I guess I felt like my only job was to be the chef here, so I had to be really good at it. I didn't mean to be so competitive."

"Me neither," Toulouse said. "I just wanted to prove myself."

"Now I understand," Marie continued. "None of us should 'own' any of the café jobs. I was afraid to ask Berlioz if I could perform, because I didn't want him to think I was trying to take over the entertainment."

"Can we just agree that we can try

whatever we want to?" Berlioz asked. "Maybe we can all be like Spike, and do things because they make us happy. Not because we want to be the best at them or because that's our one thing."

"I agree!" Marie said.

Toulouse smiled. "Me too."

They went together through the door to the café. Inside, Pierre was struggling to serve a mama duck and her seven ducklings, all in a line behind her, waiting at the pastry case.

"Looks like Pierre needs some help," Marie said. She took a step, then stopped. "Hey, Berlioz. Why don't you go over and lend a paw? You're so good at talking up everything on the menu!"

Berlioz smiled. "No problem. And,

you know, we're going to need some entertainment in a few minutes. Would you sing a song with me?"

"I would love to!" Marie exclaimed with a purr. "But first, I have some cupcakes to finish. Toulouse, would you like to come help me? I'll show you how to frost them so the icing makes a perfect swirl on top. . . ." Then Marie raised one eyebrow. "I mean, it would be fun to do something together that's not me chasing you."

"You mean *me* chasing *you*," Toulouse said, correcting her.

Marie rolled her eyes but then smiled. "That too."

Toulouse smiled back. "Sure. Let's show everyone what you and I can do as a team."

As Berlioz stepped behind the counter and greeted the mama duck, Toulouse followed Marie into the kitchen, purring, with his tail held high.

Country Days Delight

Tropical Adventure Treats

**Jennifer Castle** is the author of over a dozen books for kids and teens, including the Butterfly Wishes series and American Girl's Girl of the Year: Blaire books. She lives in New Paltz, New York, with her family, which includes five cats, a leopard gecko, and, often, a few rescued foster kittens, who are all likely planning their own creature café when the humans aren't looking.

**Sydney Hanson** is a children's book illustrator living in Sierra Madre, California. Her illustrations reflect her growing up with numerous pets and brothers in Minnesota, and her love of animals and nature. She illustrates using both traditional and digital media; her favorites are watercolor and colored pencil. When she's not drawing, she enjoys running, baking, and exploring the woods with her family. To see her latest animals and illustrations, follow her on Instagram at @sydwiki.